**"Come see! A parrot!** There's a parrot by our tree house! And he talks and everything!'' cried Titus breathlessly.

''Where?'' asked his mother, looking up at the tree.

''Right there on the branch!'' said Titus.

''I don't see it,'' said his father.

Titus turned to point to it. But the branch was empty. The parrot was gone.

Here's a new mystery for the T.C.D.C.

THE MYSTERY OF THE

# TATTLETALE PARROT

*Elspeth Campbell Murphy*
*Illustrated by Chris Wold Dyrud*

**Chariot Books**
David C. Cook Publishing Co.

A Wise Owl Book
Published by Chariot Books,
an imprint of David C. Cook Publishing Co.
David C. Cook Publishing Co., Elgin, Illinois 60120
David C. Cook Publishing Co., Weston, Ontario

The Mystery of the Tattletale Parrot
© 1988 by Elspeth Campbell Murphy for text and Chris Wold
Dyrud for illustrations

Cover design by Chris Patchel
First Printing, 1988
Printed in the United States of America
93 92 91 90 89 88 5 4 3 2 1


Library of Congress Cataloging-in-Publication Data
Murphy, Elspeth Campbell.
    The mystery of the tattletale parrot; illustrated by Chris Wold
Dyrud.
        p.      cm. — (The Ten commandments mysteries)
    Summary: In solving the mystery of who owns a parrot who has
been taught to misuse God's name in swearing, three cousins
uncover a burglary ring and experience the meaning of the
commandment, ''You shall not misuse the name of the Lord your
God.''
ISBN 1-55513-528-5
    [1. Ten commandments—Fiction. 2. Parrots—Fiction. 3.
Swearing—Fiction. 4. Cousins—Fiction. 5. Mystery and detective
stories.] I. Dyrud, Chris Wold, ill. II. Title. III. Series: Murphy,
Elspeth Campbell. Ten commandments mysteries.
PZ7.M95316Myk  1988   [Fic.]   87-26460

"You shall not misuse the name of the Lord your God."

*Exodus 20:7 (NIV)*

# CONTENTS

# CONTENTS

# 1
# IN THE TREE HOUSE

It was a lazy, leafy summer's day, and the three cousins, Timothy Dawson, Titus McKay, and Sarah-Jane Cooper, were eating lunch in Titus's tree house.

The tree house wasn't in Titus's yard. Titus lived in a high-rise apartment building downtown, so he didn't have a yard of his own. But his granduncle and grandaunt lived in a quiet, older neighborhood in the city. Granduncle Frank had built the tree house especially for Titus to play in whenever he came over.

Today Titus had his two cousins with him. Timothy was visiting Titus from the suburbs. And Sarah-Jane was visiting Titus from the country. The tree house was even more fun with company, Titus decided. He and his cousins lay back and looked up at the leaves dancing against the bright blue sky. They talked about this and that.

Sarah-Jane said, "Ti, tell me again who Granduncle Frank and Grandaunt Barbara are."

"They're my father's aunt and uncle," explained Titus patiently. "So they're my *grand*aunt and *grand*uncle. They're sort of like grandparents to me, because my real grandparents died when my father was still a kid. He came to live with his mother's brother, Uncle Frank, and his Uncle Frank's wife, Aunt Barbara."

Sarah-Jane said, "But they're not related to Tim and me, right?"

"Right," said Titus. "Because you're related to me on my *mother's* side, and they're related to me on my *father's* side."

"But we can still call them 'Grandaunt' and 'Granduncle,' can't we?" asked Sarah-Jane.

"Sure," said Titus. "They want you to."

Timothy joined in the conversation. "Besides, if we called them by their *last* name, it would be too confusing, because their *last* name is Titus—Frank and Barbara Titus. And Ti's *first* name is

10

Titus."

"That's because I'm named after them," said Titus. "My dad loved his Uncle Frank and Aunt Barbara a lot. So when I was born, he gave me their *last* name for my *first* name."

Sarah-Jane added, "And your mom says that when Granduncle Frank and Grandaunt Barbara heard what your name was going to be, they were so happy they cried."

"Yeah," said Titus. "I'm glad I'm named after them. Most people think I'm named after the Titus in the Bible. But that's OK. It's nice having a Bible person's name, too."

"I'm named after the Timothy in the Bible," said Timothy. "And my baby sister is named after a lady in the Bible called Priscilla."

"There's a Sarah in the Bible," said Sarah-Jane. "But I'm named after you guys' mothers—Tim's mother, Aunt Sarah, and Ti's mother, Aunt Jane. My mom has a book that tells what names mean. *Sarah* means 'princess.' And *Jane* means the same thing as *John*—'Jehovah has been gracious.' *Jehovah* is the Old Testament name for God."

Timothy said, "My Sunday school teacher told me that *Timothy* means 'honoring God.' "

"What?"

"I said, 'honoring God,' " repeated Timothy.

"I didn't say anything," said Titus.

"Me neither," said Sarah-Jane.

They were all quiet for a while, just looking at the leaves and the sky.

## 2
# THE VISITOR

"What?"

"I didn't say anything," said Timothy sleepily.

"Me neither," said Titus.

"Me neither," said Sarah-Jane.

"What?"

"Nothing!" said Timothy.

"I didn't say a word!" exclaimed Sarah-Jane. "Quit saying 'what?' all the time."

"I didn't say anything," said Titus. "But one of you guys keeps asking 'what?' "

"Not me," said Timothy.

"Not me," said Sarah-Jane.

"Well, *someone* must have said 'what?' " muttered Titus. "Unless we're all going crazy and hearing things. . . ."

"Poor sweet baby. Poor sweet baby. Good morning. What? Hello, there."

The cousins scrambled up and looked about them wildly.

They saw a bright green parrot, perched on a branch just outside the tree house.

Without stopping to gather up their lunch stuff, Timothy, Titus, and Sarah-Jane skidded down the tree house ladder and raced across the lawn.

"Granduncle Frank! Granduncle Frank! Come see! A *parrot*! There's a parrot by our tree house! And he talks and everything! Grandaunt Barbara!

Mom! Dad! Come see the parrot!''

The grown-ups came hurrying out the back door to see what all the commotion was about. Even Wags, Granduncle Frank's lazybones old dog, waddled out.

"*A parrot*!" cried Titus breathlessly.

"Where?" asked his mother, looking up at the tree.

"Right there on the branch!" said Titus.

"I don't see it," said his father.

Titus turned to point to it. But the branch was empty. The parrot was gone.

"Oh, no! He was right there!" cried Timothy.

"Where did he go?" asked Sarah-Jane.

Then, suddenly, they all saw a flash of green. The parrot was *in the tree house*! He was eating a leftover banana from lunch.

"Dad! Can we catch him?" asked Titus. "Can we keep him?"

"We can try to catch him," said his father. "But we can't keep him. We have to find out who he belongs to."

"How are you going to catch him?" asked Timothy. "If you come after him, he might fly away."

"Yes," said Sarah-Jane. "And if you try to pick him up, he might bite."

"It's too bad we don't have a door on the tree-

16

house," said Titus. "Then we could just close it—and we would have an instant birdcage!"

"That's just what I was thinking," said Granduncle Frank, with a wink. "I guess we Tituses think alike."

The cousins watched as Titus's dad and granduncle got some chicken wire from the shed and nailed it quickly across the entrance to the tree house.

Instant birdcage.

"EXcellent!" declared Titus.

"Neat-O!" agreed Timothy.

"Sorry you won't be able to use your tree house for a while, Titus," said Granduncle Frank.

"That's OK," said Titus. "The parrot can stay there *for as long as he wants*!"

The parrot seemed to feel the same way about it. He was more interested in the banana than in the people.

Granduncle Frank slipped a shallow bowl between the wooden slats of the tree house. Then he filled the dish up with water from a long-stemmed watering can.

"Well, he seems fine for now," Granduncle Frank said. "He's really pretty tame. But the tree house won't hold him for long. Eventually he'll chew right through the wood."

Grandaunt Barbara said, "Then we'd better get busy calling around to see if we can find the owner. I'm sure someone's reported him missing. People get upset if their pets are lost."

"Yes!" said Titus's mother. "And besides that—parrots are very expensive. If you lost one, it would be like losing a lot of money."

"Mom," said Titus, "while you're finding out who the parrot belongs to, can we climb up and talk to him?"

"I don't see why not," said Titus's mother. "I'm sure your little feathered friend would like some company."

"Not so little!" said Titus's father as the parrot let out some wild, jungle screeches.

"I could teach him not to screech," said Titus hopefully.

"No one can teach a parrot not to screech," said his father. "Let's find that owner. Now."

18

# 4
# PEPPY

So the grown-ups and Wags went back in the house, and the cousins climbed the tree. This time everything was exactly the opposite. This time the *parrot* was in the tree house eating lunch, and the *cousins* were sitting on the branches outside.

The parrot cocked his head and looked at them thoughtfully. "Peppy's a good boy," he said.

"Peppy!" exclaimed Sarah-Jane. "Is that your name—Peppy?"

"What?" asked the parrot.

"I said—Is Peppy your name?"

"What?"

"Peppy! Peppy! Is your name Peppy?"

"What?"

"I SAID—"

"Never mind, S-J," said Titus. "I think he can hear you OK. He just likes the sound of the word 'what?' Don't you, Peppy?"

"What?"

"See what I mean?"

"Poor sweet baby," said Peppy.

"Yes, you *are* a poor, sweet baby," said Sarah-Jane. "And we're going to find your owners. And they'll come and take you back to your own house. Won't that be nice?"

"Good morning."

Timothy said, "I think the owner is a woman. I heard somewhere that parrots don't just copy the words. They copy people's voices, too. And Peppy talks in a lady's voice—even if he still sounds kind of parroty."

"Good thinking, Tim!" said Titus.

But just then Peppy said in a man's voice, a worried voice, "Oh, my God! Oh, my God!"

"Did you hear what he *said*?" squeaked Sarah-Jane.

"I can't believe my ears!" said Timothy. "A *swearing parrot*!"

"Peppy!" said Titus sternly. "You're not sup-

posed to say God's name that way."

"Poor sweet baby," said Peppy.

"Well, all right," said Titus. "I guess you don't know any better. I guess you just picked it up from somewhere."

Peppy bobbed his head up and down as if he were agreeing with Titus. Again he said the same words in the worried man's voice. Then, in a different man's voice (a crabby one this time), he answered himself: "Quit worrying!"

The cousins looked at one another in bewilderment. "What's that all about?" asked Titus.

# 5
# WHAT A BIRD

Then Peppy said in his usual lady voice, "Suppertime!"

"It's not suppertime. It's lunchtime," said Timothy. "And you just finished our bananas."

"Are you still hungry, Peppy?" asked Sarah-Jane.

"What?"

"I said—Are you still hungry?"

"What?"

"I SAID—"

"S-J!" cried Timothy and Titus together.

"Oops! Sorry!" said Sarah-Jane. "I keep forgetting that Peppy likes the word 'what?' "

"What?" asked Peppy.

"I said—I keep forgetting that you like the wor— Oh, honestly, Peppy. You can be very annoying.''

"Peppy's a good boy. Suppertime! Suppertime!''

"Let's go get him some more to eat," said Timothy. "Good-bye, Peppy. We'll be back soon.''

"Bye-bye, Peppy," said Sarah-Jane. "Bye-bye, birdie!''

"Say 'good-bye,' Peppy," said Titus.

"Hello, there!" said Peppy.

When the cousins came in the back door, they heard Grandaunt Barbara on the phone.

"Thanks, anyway," she was saying. "Call us if you hear anything.''

She sighed as she hung up the phone. "I don't know where else to try," she said. "I've called the police, the humane society, the newspapers, the animal hospital, the pet stores, even the zoo. No one has reported a missing parrot.''

"Well, the parrot can't have flown here from *too* far away," said Granduncle Frank. "I noticed his wings were clipped."

"Oh, no!" cried Sarah-Jane.

"It's all right, Sweetheart," said Granduncle Frank kindly. "Clipping a bird's wings doesn't hurt the bird at all. In fact, it's supposed to help by keeping the bird from flying away and getting lost."

Grandaunt Barbara said, "Unfortunately, this bird got lost anyway. I think we should put our own ad in the newspaper: Found—one lost, green parrot."

"Whose name is Peppy," added Timothy.

"Oh, good," said Titus's dad. "You found out his name. Too bad the owners didn't teach him his address and phone number, too.''

Sarah-Jane said, ''Maybe he knows them, but he just hasn't said them yet. Peppy says a lot of things besides his name. He says, 'Peppy's a good boy,' and 'Poor sweet baby' and 'Supper-time' and 'Good morning' and 'Hello, there' and 'What?'—that's his favorite word. And he swears, too.''

The grown-ups looked at one another in alarm. ''What does he say?'' asked Titus's mother.

Titus answered quickly, ''He doesn't say any dirty words or anything like that. But he doesn't use God's name the right way—like you do when you're praying.''

''He uses God's name carelessly, you mean,'' said Granduncle Frank. ''And that's against the commandment that says, 'You shall not misuse the name of the Lord your God.' But, of course, Peppy doesn't know what he's saying. He's just repeating what he's heard. People shouldn't swear at all—and especially not around parrots! You never know what a good talker will pick up.''

Titus asked, ''Is it a different kind of swearing

when they say in court, 'Do you swear to tell the truth, the whole truth, and nothing but the truth, so help you God?' "

Granduncle Frank said, "When someone swears in court, he's actually making a promise—a promise to tell the truth. It's like he's saying, 'This is so serious, I'm calling on God to back up what I tell you.' "

"But then what if the person lies?" asked Titus.

"Then he has misused God's name," said Granduncle Frank.

Titus's mother said, "God's name is important to Him, just as our names are important to us, Titus. If you use a person's name in the wrong way, you're saying you don't respect him. I remember when I was a little girl. There was this mean kid in my class, who didn't like me. And whenever she saw me, she'd yell, "Jane, Jane! You give me a pain!"

"That's terrible!" said Sarah-Jane.

"Yes," said her aunt. "It really hurt my feelings. But I'll tell you what made me feel *wonderful*." She gave Sarah-Jane a hug. "It was when your mom named her baby girl after Timothy's mother and me. My sister Sue honored me—and honored my name."

"We know how good that feels!" said Grandaunt Barbara. And she beamed at Titus.

"So," said Granduncle Frank, "that's why we honor God's name instead of misusing it."

"You know," said Titus casually. "If Peppy came to live with us, I could teach him not to swear."

His mother laughed. "Nice try, kid! But we *have* to find the owners. I can't imagine why no

27

one is looking for Peppy. We didn't have any luck with our phone calling, so now it's up to the T.C.D.C.''

# 7
# THE T.C.D.C.

"What's a 'teesy-deesy'?" asked Granduncle Frank and Grandaunt Barbara.

"It's letters," explained Timothy.

"Capital T.

Capital C.

Capital D.

Capital C.

It stands for the Three Cousins Detective Club."

"That sounds like exactly the help we need," said Granduncle Frank. "Can Wags and I be honorary members today? We thought we'd go door to door in the neighborhood and just ask people if they're missing a parrot."

"Sure! We can help with that!" said Titus. "But first, we promised Peppy we'd get him some more food."

Grandaunt Barbara said, "When I talked to the man at the pet store, he said most parrots love peanuts. I happen to have some peanuts on hand for a new recipe, but—anything for Peppy!"

The cousins hurried back to the tree house with the peanuts.

"We're back, Peppy," said Timothy. "But we can't stay. We have to go find your owners. You can depend on the T.C.D.C.!"

"What?"

"The T.C.D.C.," said Timothy.

"The T.C.D.C.," said Titus.

"The T.C.D.C.," said Sarah-Jane.

But Peppy didn't look very impressed. He was too busy eating peanuts.

The cousins and Granduncle Frank began their search by being on the lookout for posters.

Granduncle Frank said, "Once, when Wags was a puppy, he ran away. So Barbara and I put up signs on the lampposts and in the store windows. Someone saw one of the signs and recognized our description of Wags. He knew it was the same puppy that had run into his yard."

"I can't imagine Wags *running* at all," said

Timothy.

Granduncle Frank laughed. ''No, he's a lazy-bones, old dog now. So, if you don't mind, we'll just wait on the sidewalk, while you kids run up to the houses.''

So the cousins went door to door. They took turns doing the talking, asking if anyone had lost a parrot.

# 8

# DOOR TO DOOR

Titus said to Timothy and Sarah-Jane, "This is just like trick-or-treating."

"Except we're not wearing costumes," said Sarah-Jane.

"And we're not yelling 'trick-or-treat,' " said Timothy.

"And no one is giving us candy," said Titus.

"And it's not shivery cold like in October," said Sarah-Jane.

"And it's in the middle of the afternoon, instead of spooky nighttime," said Timothy.

"Come to think of it," said Titus, "this isn't like trick-or-treating at all. And—it's getting really BOR-ING."

Timothy and Sarah-Jane had to agree that he was right.

When they had first started out, they had been so sure that they would find Peppy's owner right away. They had gone up to each new house full of hope that this would be the one. But then they had come back to Granduncle Frank and Wags full of disappointment. *No one* was missing a parrot.

They were just about ready to give up, when they came to a lady who said, "Don't talk to me about parrots! The woman next door has one. *Screech, screech, screech!* Come to think of it, I haven't heard it for a day or two. I don't know how she got it to stop screeching. But I sure hope it doesn't start up again."

As they hurried next door, Titus said, "I think we're onto something. If that neighbor hasn't heard the parrot screeching, it must be because it's gone. I think we're about to find Peppy's owner at last!"

At first the lady at the next house looked at them very suspiciously. But then she said, "Oh, maybe something wonderful has happened! Maybe Perry has escaped! Wait here, children. I'll just get a bird carrier and be right with you."

"This is very strange," said Titus, as they waited for the lady to come back. "Why would she be *glad* her parrot had escaped?"

"And why did she call him *Perry*?" asked Timothy. "I thought his name was Peppy."

But they didn't have time to talk about it anymore. The lady was back and eager to go with them and Granduncle Frank to the tree house.

"We're back, poor sweet baby," Sarah-Jane called out to the bird. (She wasn't sure whether to keep calling him Peppy or start calling him Perry.)

"The T.C.D.C. found your owner," said Titus.

"You can depend on the T.C.D.C.!" said Timothy.

The lady climbed the tree house ladder as fast as she could (which wasn't very fast). But she came right back down. Her eyes were filled with tears.

"That's not Perry," she said.

# 9
# THE NOTE

Grandaunt Barbara brought out lemonade and cookies. And the lady, whose name was Mrs. Johnson, told them the whole, sad story.

"I just got Perry," she said. "In fact, he's not even mine. He belongs to a friend, who's on a long ocean cruise. My friend is very rich. I could never afford a bird like Perry. He's a Hyacinth Macaw—very rare. Very beautiful, with gorgeous, purplish-blue feathers.

"Anyway, Perry knows me. And my friend knew I would love taking care of him. I took care of a lot of birds when I worked in a pet store. So my friend gave my name and address to the breeder where she got Perry—and the idea was that I could call the breeder anytime I had any questions.

"Well, Perry and I were getting along beautifully until—until the day before yesterday. I came home from shopping and found that someone had broken in and *taken* Perry. Nothing else was gone—just the macaw. Oh, what am I going to do?"

"I don't understand," said Greataunt Barbara. "Why haven't you reported him missing?"

"Because of *this*," said Mrs. Johnson. And she pulled a note out of her pocket.

They all crowded around to read it.

It was a ransom note.

Titus said, "You mean Perry has been kidnapped—I mean, birdnapped?"

Mrs. Johnson nodded miserably. "They say they want a thousand dollars. I don't *have* a thousand dollars. They say if I don't pay up or if I go to the police, I'll never see Perry again."

"I'm sure they won't hurt him," said Titus's mother gently. "The worst that can happen is that they'll sell him to someone else. You said that a Hyacinth is rare. Is it very expensive?"

Mrs. Johnson nodded. She looked like she could hardly keep from crying. "They're one of the most expensive kinds. My friend paid over $6,000 for Perry.''

''Whoa!'' cried Timothy. ''I can see why they birdnapped him!''

Titus was thinking hard. ''We're forgetting about *Peppy*,'' he said. ''Maybe he was bird-napped, too. And—maybe he escaped from his birdnappers. We know he couldn't fly very far. That means the birdnappers must be someplace around here. I say we keep going door to door—but this time, we'll be on the lookout for some-thing suspicious.''

''I'm with Titus,'' said Timothy.

''You can count on us—the T.C.D.C.!'' said Sarah-Jane.

''I know we can,'' said Granduncle Frank. ''But Mrs. Johnson really should go to the police about Perry.''

''I know you're right, Mr. Titus,'' said Mrs. Johnson. ''But I'm so afraid I'll never see Perry again if I do.''

''Couldn't we look just a little longer—maybe an hour or so?'' begged Titus.

''All right,'' said Granduncle Frank.

The cousins felt more determined than ever.
They had *two* birds to worry about now. And they
had only an hour to get to the bottom of things.

So they went door to door again, with Granduncle Frank, Mrs. Johnson, and Wags following
along.

When the hour was almost up, they came to a
house kind of set off by itself, next to a vacant
lot. A stereo was blaring from inside.

"Why do people need to play the music that
loud?" complained Granduncle Frank.

Everyone was feeling a little tired and crabby.

It was hot.

The afternoon was growing late.

And they hadn't had any luck.

Timothy, Titus, and Sarah-Jane trudged up to the house. They had to ring the doorbell several times and bang on the door.

Finally, a nervous-looking young man came to the door. He looked even more nervous when he found out what they wanted.

"Parrots?" he said. "No, no. I don't know anything about parrots." And he quickly shut the door.

As they turned to leave, Timothy noticed something on the ground at the side of the house. He went to check it out. His cousins followed him.

They were standing near an open window.

So they heard clearly when the young man said, in a very worried voice, the same words Peppy had used. And they also heard clearly when *another* man answered him in a crabby voice, "Quit worrying!"

The cousins raced back to Granduncle Frank and Mrs. Johnson.

"The birdnappers!" Titus gasped. "We heard them talking just now. And they sounded just like Peppy!"

"And look what I found in the yard!" said Timothy. He held out a beautiful, purplish-blue feather.

"*Perry*!" cried Mrs. Johnson. "They have *Perry* in there!" And before anyone could stop her, she hurried toward the house. Granduncle Frank went after her.

Just then Sarah-Jane spotted a police car at the other end of the street. She and the boys ran as fast as they could go, waving their arms and yelling, "Help, police! Help! Help!"

"In here!" they said, leading the police to the house.

Mrs. Johnson met them at the door. She was holding Perry in her arms and cooing to calm him down. "The men got away," she said. "As soon as they heard us coming, they went out the back door and drove away. But at least the birds are all right."

"*Birds*?!" said the policemen. "Suppose you tell us what's going on here."

So Granduncle Frank explained about the birdnapping plan. One whole room of the house was used just for the birds. There was a cockatoo, a scarlet macaw, and two more parrots. There was also an empty cage. Probably the one Peppy escaped from, the cousins thought.

"Now I know why they had the stereo turned up so loud," said Granduncle Frank. "It was to cover all this squawking and screeching."

The police found a list of the birds and their owners.

"Now I see what those guys did," said the first policeman. "It looks like they were able to steal a list of the breeder's customers. That way they knew who owned these valuable birds—and where they lived.''

"Don't worry," said the second policeman. "We'll get these guys. And we'll see that the birds get back to their rightful owners.''

"Is *Peppy* on that list?'' asked Sarah-Jane.

He certainly was.

Granduncle Frank said, "Peppy's owners aren't from this part of town after all. But it's still a good thing you kids did all that hard, door-to-door detective work. That's how we found out about *Perry*. And that's how we found the birdnappers.''

Peppy's owner was a very nice lady named Miss Kingsley. She was overjoyed to get him back.

She said, "Oh, I was so frantic! I didn't know *what* to do.''

"I know *exactly* how you feel," said Mrs. Johnson.

The two bird lovers began talking together like old friends. And they each thanked the cousins seven million times for getting their parrots back.

Granduncle Frank said, "Um, Miss Kingsley—I'm afraid Peppy picked up some swearing from the birdnappers."

"Oh, dear!" said Miss Kingsley. "It's going to be so hard to teach him not to do that. What a bird! I can't get him to learn 'good-bye'—but he learns how to swear!"

"But look at it this way," said Titus. "That's how he tattled on the birdnappers! He's one smart bird!"

"Peppy's a good boy," added Peppy.

"Of course, you are," said Miss Kingsley,

laughing. "Now, can you say 'good-bye' to the children?"

Peppy cocked his head to one side and looked at them thoughtfully.

"Oh, please don't say 'what?' again," said Sarah-Jane.

But Peppy had picked up something new. And the cousins couldn't believe their ears.

"Teesy-deesy," said Peppy happily. "Teesy-deesy. Teesy-deesy. Teesy-deesy."

## The End

# THE TEN COMMANDMENTS MYSTERIES

When Timothy, Titus, and Sarah-Jane, the three cousins, get together the most ordinary events turn into mysteries. So they've formed the T.C.D.C. (That's the Three Cousins Detective Club.)

And while the three cousins are solving mysteries, they're also learning about the Ten Commandments and living God's way.

### *You'll want to solve all ten mysteries along with Sarah-Jane, Ti, and Tim:*

The Mystery of the Laughing Cat—"You shall not steal." *Someone stole rare coins. Can the cousins find the thief?*

The Mystery of the Messed-up Wedding—"You shall not commit adultery." *Can the cousins find the missing wedding ring?*

The Mystery of the Gravestone Riddle—"You shall not murder." *Can the cousins solve a 100-year-old murder case?*

The Mystery of the Carousel Horse—"You shall not covet." *Why does the stranger want an old, wooden horse?*

The Mystery of the Vanishing Present—"Remember the Sabbath day and keep it holy." *Can the cousins figure out who has Grandpa's missing birthday gift?*

The Mystery of the Silver Dolphin—"You shall not give false testimony." *Who's telling the truth—and who's lying?*

The Mystery of the Tattletale Parrot—"You shall not misuse the name of the Lord your God." *What will the beautiful green parrot say next?*

The Mystery of the Second Map—"You shall have no other gods before me." *Can the cousins discover who dropped the strange map?*

The Mystery of the Double Trouble—"Honor your father and your mother." *How could Timothy be in two places at once?*

The Mystery of the Silent Idol—"You shall not make for yourself an idol." *If the idol could speak, what would it tell the cousins?*

### *Available at your local Christian bookstore.*

David C. Cook Publishing Co., Elgin, IL 60120

# SHOELACES AND BRUSSELS SPROUTS

## One little lie, but BIG trouble!

When Alex lies to her mom about losing her shoelaces, it doesn't seem like a big deal. But how do you replace special baseball laces when you don't have any money and you're not allowed to go to the store alone? A big softball game is coming up, and Alex knows the coach won't let her pitch in shoes without laces—or in cowboy boots!

Every kid gets into the predicaments that Alex does—ones that start out small and mushroom. Readers will learn from Alex's mistakes and understand that they have the same sources of help that she turns to: A God who loves them and wants to help them, and parents who understand.

*Other books in the Alex Series . . .*

2 *French Fry Forgiveness*—Sometimes making friends is harder than making enemies.

3 *Hot Chocolate Friendship*—Is winning first place as important to Alex as being a friend?

4 *Peanut Butter and Jelly Secrets*—Obeying her parents (even in little things) beats the awful results of disobeying.

*Available at your local Christian bookstore.*

David C. Cook Publishing Co.
850 N. Grove Ave.
Elgin, IL 60120

Chariot Books